Jane's Precious Jewel

Written By
Val Pugh-Love

Illustrated By
Willie A. Love, II

Printed in the United States of America.
First Printing, 2015
ISBN: 978-0-692-54429-7
Val Pugh, LLC
Shreveport, LA 71129
www.valpughlove.com

Dedication

Thank you for sharing *Jane's Precious Jewel*
with your child. This book was written in
honor of my maternal grandmother,
Jane Ann Louis and in loving memory of
my maternal great-grandmother, our
"Precious Jewel"

Annie Lee Gay Lister
(October 5, 1921 - October 15, 2010).

My prayer is that your family will be
encouraged to cherish your precious jewels
as they continue to shine brightly in your
lives – even if they have gone on to
"Jewel Heaven."

"Hi, Mommy," Jane says sadly.

"Hi, Jane. What's wrong, honey?"

"I can't find my jewel," Jane says.

"Aww, darling. Maybe you left it at the church," Mom says. "I saw you with it on Sunday."

"I think you're right! May I go look for my jewel at the church?!" Jane exclaims.

"I suppose it won't hurt if you do, but hurry back," Mom says.

Jane hurries off to search for her jewel.
She skips and whistles for two blocks until
she reaches her family's church.

CHURCH

"Hi, Bishop!" Jane says to the pastor of her family's church.

"Hello, Jane! What brings you here today?" Bishop asks as he continues to hammer a loose board on the floor.

"I lost my jewel, and I think I may have left it here," Jane yells over Bishop's loud hammering.

Bishop stops hammering and asks, "What does this jewel look like?"

3

Jane's face lights up as she describes her jewel.

"It's small, colorful, and shiny! My precious jewel is special to me, and I take it everywhere I go."

"I see," Bishop says as he tries to picture Jane's jewel. "Name a few of the places you have taken your precious jewel."

A bright smile appears on Jane's face as she names the places she has travelled with her jewel.

"My jewel and I have gone many places with my family, including the Martin Luther King, Jr. Memorial in Atlanta, Georgia. We have been to Oakland, California to see our family, and we've even been to New Orleans, Louisiana!"

"Wow!" Bishop exclaims. "You and your precious jewel sure do like to travel! I really wish I knew where you left your jewel. Have you asked your friends if they have seen it?"

GEORGIA

LOUISIANA

CALIFORNIA

Jane remembers having her jewel with her when she was at her next door neighbors' house. *Bishop may be right.* Jane thinks to herself. "That's a great idea. I need to go ask my mom if I can check with my friends," Jane says.

"Thanks, Bishop!" Jane says as she quickly runs home to ask her mom if she can check with her friends.

Jane runs into the kitchen where her mom is doing some cleaning.

"Mom, mom!" Jane is so excited that she startles her mother.

"What is it, Jane?!" Mom asks in a worried tone.

"Bishop has not seen my jewel, but he thinks Chandler and Chase may have seen it. Is it okay if I go next door to check with them?" Jane asks.

Mom relaxes when she realizes everything is okay.

"Sure, Jane, but I need you to calm down, honey. You made me think something terrible happened."

Jane feels bad about scaring her mother.

"I'm sorry, Mom. It's just that my jewel is so precious to me, and losing it has me so sad. I need to find it!"

Mom hugs Jane.

"Okay, sweetheart. Go check with Chandler and Chase. Maybe they have seen your jewel."

Jane hurries to her neighbors' house.

Jane is greeted by Ms. Ann as she knocks on her neighbors' door.

"Hi, Ms. Ann. Are Chandler and Chase home?" Jane asks.

"Hi, Jane. Yes, they are. They will be right out," Ms. Ann says as she calls for her sons who are busy playing their video game. "Boys, Jane is here to see you."

Chandler and Chase turn off their video game and come running to see their favorite next door neighbor.

"Hi, Jane," Chandler says as he grabs his blue skateboard.

"What's up, Jane?" Chase says as he plays with his toy truck.

"Hi, guys. I was just wondering if you have seen my jewel," Jane asks hoping that her search is finally over.

"What kind of jewel?" Chandler asks, as he does a cool trick on his skateboard.

Before Jane can answer, Chase says, "I know which jewel she means. She has a really cool jewel that she takes everywhere she goes. I'm sorry, Jane. I have not seen your jewel."

Chandler says, "I haven't seen it either, but tell me more about your jewel."

Jane feels so lost without her jewel.

"Ohhh nooo!" she exclaims. "I'll never find my jewel. It's really shiny, colorful, pretty, and precious. It makes me feel safe. That's why I take it everywhere with me. I just can't seem to find it anywhere!"

Chandler feels sad for Jane and gives her an idea.

"I'm sorry we couldn't help, but maybe you will find it if you stop looking for it."

Chandler's idea makes no sense to Chase, and Chase lets him know it.

15

"What do you mean? If she stops looking for it, she will never find it!"

Jane, however, likes Chandler's idea.

"Just a second, Chase," Jane says. " Maybe Chandler is right. Sometimes I do find things that I haven't seen in a long time, even when I'm not looking for them. Thanks for your help, guys. I have to go home so I won't be late for dinner."

Jane decides to end her search for the night. Chase and Chandler play outside a little longer until their mom is finished cooking their dinner.

"Bye, Jane. We'll see you later," the boys say in unison as Jane hurries home.

"I'm home, Mom," Jane says.

"Hello, sweetheart. Did you have any luck finding your jewel?" Mom asks.

"No, I did not," Jane replies, "but, Chandler gave me an idea. He said I may find my jewel if I stop looking for it. As much as I want to keep looking for it, I am going to stop for now."

"I know you really want to find your jewel, but I agree with Chandler. I'm sure it is in a very special place. When the Lord wants you to see your jewel again, you will know it," Mom says as she finishes cooking dinner.

Jane is not sure what her mother means. *Did God take my jewel?* Jane thinks to herself.

""What do you mean?" Jane asks.

"Well, sweetie, sometimes God needs to use our precious jewels for special reasons. He lets us borrow them for a while, then He takes our precious jewels to a special place," Mom says hoping to cheer Jane up.

Really?" Jane thinks for a second and prays silently. "God, please take good care of my jewel and return it to me."

Jane finishes her dinner and hurries upstairs to take a bath before she goes to bed.

"I'm all done, Mommy!" Jane says as she goes to her room and hops into her bed.

"Jane, I'm sorry you didn't find your jewel today. When you say your prayers tonight, ask God to help you find your jewel. I'm sure this will work. Goodnight, sweetie," Mom says as she gives Jane a kiss.

"Goodnight, Mommy," Jane says.

Jane lies in bed and looks at the stars through her bedroom window. As she thinks about her jewel, she sees one star shining brighter than all the others. This star is even brighter than the North Star. Plus, it's shiny, colorful, and precious just like Jane's jewel.

Jane hurries to her window to get a closer look. Suddenly, she realizes that the special star really is her jewel! Jane thinks back to what her mother said about God taking jewels to a special place. *God has my jewel*, she thinks to herself as she gets back into her bed with a big smile.

When Jane says her prayers, she thanks God for her precious jewel and all the fun things they were able to do together.

25

Suddenly, the star twinkles just as Jane finishes saying her prayers. Seeing the twinkling star makes her feel special, and she knows that God has heard her prayer. Jane falls asleep with a big smile on her face, while her precious *star* shines even brighter!